THE ISLE OF PIRATE'S DOOM

BY

ROBERT E. HOWARD

British Library Cataloguing-in-Publication Data
A catalogue record for this book is available from the
British Library

Contents

Robert E. Howard

Robert Ervin Howard was born in Peaster, Texas in 1906. During his youth, his family moved between a variety of Texan boomtowns, and Howard – a bookish and somewhat introverted child – was steeped in the violent myths and legends of the Old South. Although he loved reading and learning, Howard developed a distinctly Texan, hardboiled outlook on the world. He became a passionate fan of boxing, taking it up at an amateur level, and from the age of nine began to write adventure tales of semi-historical bloodshed. In 1919, when Howard was thirteen, his family moved to the Central Texas hamlet of Cross Plains, where he would stay for the rest of his life.

At fifteen Howard began to read the pulp magazines of the day, and to write more seriously. The December 1922 issue of his high school newspaper featured two of his stories, 'Golden Hope Christmas' and 'West is West'. In 1924 he sold his first piece – a short caveman tale titled 'Spear and Fang' – for $16 to the not-yet-famous *Weird Tales* magazine. He published with the magazine regularly over the next few years. 1929 was a breakout year for Howard, in that the 23-year-old writer began to sell to other magazines, such as *Ghost Stories* and *Argosy*, both of whom had previously sent him hundreds of rejection slips. In 1930, he began a correspondence with weird fiction master H. P. Lovecraft which ran up to his death six years later, and is regarded as one of the great correspondence cycles in all of fantasy literature.

It was partly due to Lovecraft's encouragement that Howard created his most famous character, Conan the Cimmerian. Conan – a barbarian-turned-King during the Hyborian Age, a mythical period of some 12,000 years ago – featured in seventeen *Weird Tales* stories between 1933 and 1936, and is now regarded as having spawned the 'sword and sorcery' genre, making Howard's influence on fantasy literature comparable to that of J. R. R. Tolkien's. The Conan stories have since been adapted many times, most famously in the series of films starring Arnold Schwarzenegger.

Howard was enjoying an all-time high in sales by the beginning of 1936, but he was also deeply upset by the ill health of his mother, who had fallen into a coma. On the morning of June 11, 1936, he asked an attending nurse whether she would ever recover, and the nurse replied negatively. Howard walked to his car, parked outside the family home in Cross Plains, and shot himself. He died eight hours later, aged just thirty.

THE FIRST DAY

The long low craft which rode off-shore had an unsavory look, and lying close in my covert, I was glad that I had not hailed her. Caution had prompted me to conceal myself and observe her crew before making my presence known, and now I thanked my guardian spirit; for these were troublous times and strange craft haunted the Caribees.

True, the scene was fair and peaceful enough. I crouched among green and fragrant bushes on the crest of a slope which ran down before me to the broad beach. Tall trees rose about me, their ranks sweeping away on either hand. Below on the shore, green waves broke on the white sand and overhead the blue sky hung like a dream. But as a viper in a verdant garden lay that sullen black ship, anchored just outside the shallow water.

She had an unkempt look, a slouchy, devil-may-care rigging which speaks not of an honest crew or a careful master. Anon rough voices floated across the intervening space of water and beach, and once I saw a great hulking fellow slouching along the rail lift something to his lips and then hurl it overboard.

Now the crew was lowering a longboat, heavily loaded with men, and as they laid hand to oar and drew away from the ship, their coarse shouts and the replies of those who remained on deck came to me though the words were vague and indistinct.

Crouching lower, I yearned for a telescope that I might learn the name of the ship, and presently the longboat swept in close to the beach. There were eight men in her: seven great rough fellows and the other a slim foppishly-clad varlet wearing a cocked hat who did no rowing. Now as they approached, I perceived that there was an argument among them. Seven of them roared and bellowed at the dandy, who, if he answered at all, spoke in a tone so low that I could not hear.

The boat shot through the light surf, and as she beached, a huge hairy rogue in the bow heaved up and plunged at the fop, who sprang up to meet him. I saw steel flash and heard the larger man bellow. Instantly, the other leapt nimbly out, splashed through the wet sand and legged it inland as fast as he might, while the other rogues streamed out in pursuit, yelling and brandishing weapons. He who had begun the brawl halted a moment to make the longboat fast, then took up the chase, cursing at the top of his bull's voice, the blood trickling down his face.

The dandy in the cocked hat led by several paces as they reached the first fringe of trees. Abruptly, he vanished into the foliage while the rest raced after him, and for a while, I could hear the alarums and bellowings of the chase, till the sounds faded in the distance.

4

Now I looked again at the ship. Her sails were filling and I could see men in the rigging. As I watched, the anchor came aboard and she stood off-and from her peak broke out the Jolly Roger. Truth, 'twas no more than I had expected.

Cautiously, I worked my way further back among the bushes on hands and knees and then stood up. A gloominess of spirit fell upon me, for when the sails had first come in sight, I had looked for rescue. But instead of proving a blessing, the ship had disgorged eight ruffians on the island for me to cope with.

Puzzled, I showly picked a way between the trees. Doubtless these buccaneers had been marooned by their comrades, a common affair with the bloody Brothers of the Main.

Nor did I know what I might do, since I was unarmed and these rogues would certainly regard me as an enemy, as in truth I was to all their ilk. My gorge rose against running and hiding from them, but I saw naught else to do. Nay, 'twould be rare fortune were I able to escape them at all.

Meditating thus, I had travelled inland a considerable distance yet had heard naught of the pirates, when I came to a small glade. 'Tall trees, crowned with lustrous green vines and gemmed with small exotic-hued birds flitting through their branches, rose about me. The musk of tropic growths filled the air and the stench of blood as well. A man lay dead in the glade.

Flat on his back he lay, his seaman's shirt drenched with the gore which had ebbed from the wound below his heart. He was one of the Brethren of the Red Account, no doubt of that. He'd never shoes to his feet, but a great ruby glimmered on his finger, and a costly silk sash girdled the waist of his tarry pantaloons. Through this sash were thrust a pair of flintlock pistols and a cutlass lay near his hand.

Here were weapons, at least. So I drew the pistols from his sash, noting they were charged, and having thrust them in my waistband, I took his cutlass, too. He would never need weapons again and I had good thought that I might very soon.

Then as I turned from despoiling the dead, a soft mocking laugh brought me round like a shot. The dandy of the longboat stood before me. Faith, he was smaller than I had thought, though supple and lithe. Boots of fine Spanish leather he wore on his trim legs, and above them tight britches of doeskin. A fine crimson sash with tassels and rings to the ends was round his slim waist, and from it jutted the silver butts of two pistols. A blue coat with flaring tails and gold buttons gaped open to disclose the frilled and laced shirt beneath. Again, I noted that the cocked hat still rode the owner's brow at a jaunty angle, golden hair showing underneath.

"Satan's throne!" said the wearer of this finery. "There is a great ruby ring you've overlooked!"

Now I looked for the first time at the face. It was a delicate oval with red lips that curled in mockery, large grey eyes that danced, and only then did I realize that I was looking at a woman and not a man. One hand rested saucily on her hip, the other held a long ornately-hilted rapier-and with a twitch of repulsion I saw a trace of blood on the blade.

"Speak, man!" cried she impatiently. "Are you not ashamed to be caught at your work?"

Now I doubt that I was a sight to inspire respect, what with my bare feet and my single garment, sailor's pantaloons, and they stained and discolored with salt water. But at her mocking tone, my anger stirred.

"At least," said I, finding my voice, "if I must answer for robbing a corpse, someone else must answer for making it."

"Ha, I struck a spark then?" she laughed in a hard way. "Satan's Fiends, if I'm to answer for all the corpses I've made, 'twill be a wearisome reckoning."

My gorge rose at that.

"One lives and one learns," said I. "I had not thought to meet a woman who rejoiced in cold-blooded murder."

"Cold-blooded, say you!" she fired up then, "Am I then to stand and be butchered like a sheep?"

"Had you chosen the proper life for a woman you had had no necessity either to slay or be slain," said I, carried away by my revulsion. And I then regretted what I had said for it was beginning to dawn on me who this girl must be.

"So, so, self-righteous," sneered she, her eyes beginning to flash dangerously, "so you think I'm a rogue! And what might you be, may I ask; what do you on this out-of-the-way island and why do you come-a-stealing through the jungle to take the belongings of dead men?"

"My name is Stephen Harmer, mate of The Blue Countess, Virginia trader. Seven days ago she burned to the waterline from a fire that broke out in her hold and all her crew perished save myself. I floated on a hatch, and eventually raised this island where I have been ever since."

The girl eyed me half-thoughtfully, half-mockingly, while I told my tale, as if expecting me to lie.

"As for taking weapons," I added, "it's but bitter mead to bide without arms among such rogues."

"Name them none of mine," she answered shortly, then even more abruptly: "Do you know who I am'?"

"There could be only one name you could wear-what with your foppery and cold-blooded manner."

"And that's-?"

"Helen Tavrel."

"I bow to your intuition," she said sardonically, "for it does not come to my mind that we have ever met."

"No man can sail the Seven Seas without hearing Helen Tavrel's name, and, to the best of my knowledge, she is the only woman pirate now roving the Caribees."

"So, you have heard the sailors' talk? And what do they say of me, then?"

"That you are as bold and heartless a creature as ever walked a quarter-deck or traded petticoats for breeches," I answered frankly.

Her eyes sparkled dangerously and she cut viciously at a flower with her sword point.

"And is that all they say?"

"They say that though you follow a vile and bloody trade, no man can say truthfully that he ever so much as kissed your lips."

This seemed to please her for she smiled.

"And do you believe that, sir?"

"Aye," I answered boldly, "though may I roast in Hades if ever I saw a pair more kissable."

For truth to tell, the rare beauty of the girl was going to my head, I who had looked on no woman for months. My heart softened toward her, then the sight of the dead man at my feet sobered me. But before I could say more, she turned her head aside as if listening.

"Come!" she exclaimed. "I think I hear Gower and his fools returning! If there is any place on this cursed island where one may hide a space, lead me there, for they will kill us both if they find us!"

Certes I could not leave her to be slaughtered, so I motioned her to follow me and made off through the trees and bushes. I struck for the southern end of the island, going swiftly but warily, the girl following as light-footed as an Indian brave. The bright-hued butterflies flitted about us and high in the interwoven branches of the thick trees sang birds of vivid plumage. But a tension was in the air as if, with the coming of the pirates, a mist of death hung over the whole island.

The underbrush thinned as we progressed and the land sloped upward, finally breaking into a number of ravines and cliffs. Among these we made our way and much I marveled at the activity of the girl, who sprang about and climbed with the ease of a cat, and even outdid me who had passed most of my life in ship's rigging.

At last we came to a low cliff which faced the south. At its foot ran a small stream of clear water, bordered by white sand and shadowed by waving fronds and tall vegetation which grew to the edge of the sand. Beyond, across this narrow rankly-grown expanse there rose other higher cliffs, fronting north and completing a natural gorge.

"We must go down this," I said, indicating the cliff on which we stood. "Let me aid you-"

But she, with a scornful toss of her head, had already let herself over the cliff's edge and was making her way down, clinging foot and hand to the long heavy vines which grew across the face of it. I started to follow, then hesitated as a movement among the fronds by the stream caught my eye. I spoke a quick word of warning-the girl looked up to catch what I had said-and then a withered vine gave way and she clutched wildly and fell sprawling. She did not fall far and the sand in which she lighted was soft, but on the instant, before she could regain her feet, the vegetation parted and a tall pirate leaped upon her.

I glimpsed in a single fleeting instant the handkerchief knotted about his skull, the snarling bearded face, the cutlass swung high in a brawny hand. No time for her to draw sword or pistol-he loomed over her like the shadow of death and the cutlass swept downward-but even as it did I drew pistol and fired blindly and without aim. He swerved sidewise, the cutlass veering wildly, and pitched face down in the sand without a sound. And so close had been her escape that the sweep of his blade had knocked the cocked hat from the girl's locks.

I fairly flung myself down the cliff and stood over the body of the buccaneer. The deed had been done involuntarily, without conscious thought, but I did not regret it. Whether the girl deserved saving from death- -a fact which I doubted-I considered it a worthy deed to rid the seas of at least one of those wolves which scoured it.

Helen was dusting her garments and cursing softly to herself because her hat was awry.

"Come," said I, somewhat vexed, "you are lucky to have escaped with a skull uncloven. Let us begone ere his comrades come up at the sound of the shot."

"That was a goodly feat," said she, preparing to follow me. "Fair through the temples you drilled him-- I doubt me if I could have done better."

"It was pure luck that guided the ball," I answered angrily, for of all faults I detest in women, heartlessness is the greatest. "I had no time to take aim-and had I had such time, I might not have fired."

This silenced her and she said no more until we reached the opposite cliffs. There at the foot stretched a long expanse of solid stone and I bade her walk upon it. So we went along the line of the cliff and presently came to a small waterfall where a stream tumbled over the cliffs edge to join the one in the gorge.

"There's a cave behind that fall," said I, speaking above the chatter of the water. "I discovered it by accident one day. Follow me."

So saying, I waded into the pool which whirled and eddied at the cliff's foot, and ducking my head, plunged through the falling sheet of water with the girl close behind.

We found ourselves in a small dark cavern which ran back until it vanished in the blackness, and in front the light ebbed in faintly through the silver screen of the falling water. This was the hiding place I had been making for when I met the girl.

f led the way back into the cavern until the sound of the falling stream died to a murmur and the girl's face glimmered like a rare white flower in the thick darkness.

"Damme," she said, beating the water from her coat with the cocked hat, "you lead me in some cursed inconvenient places, Mr. Harmer; first, I fall in the sand and soil my garments, and now they are wet. Will not Gower and his gang follow the sound of the pistol shot and find us, tracking our footprints where we bent down the bushes crossing from cliff to cliff?"

"No doubt they will come," I answered, "but they will be able to track us only to the cliff where we walked a good way on stone which shows no footprint. They will not know whether we went up or down or whither. There's not one chance in a hundred of them ever discovering this cavern. At any rate, it's the safest place on the island for us."

"Do you still wish you had let Dick Comrel kill me?" she asked.

"He was a bloody pirate, whatever his name might be," I replied. "No, you're too comely for such a death, no matter what your crimes."

"Your compliments take the sting from your accusations, but your accusations rob your compliments of their sweetness. Do you really hate me?"

"No, not you, but the red trade you follow. Were you in some other walk of life it's joyed I'd be to look on you."

"Zounds," said she, "but you are a strange fellow. One moment you talk like a courtier and the next like a chaplain. What really are your feelings that you speak so inconsistently?"

"I am fascinated and repelled," I replied, for the dim white oval of her face floated before me and her nearness made my senses reel. "As a woman, you attract me, but, as a pirate, you rouse a loathing in me. God's truth, but you are a very monster, like that Lilith of old, with the face of a beautiful maiden and the body of a serpent."

Her soft laugh lilted silvery and mocking in the shadows.

"So, so, broad-brim. You saved my life, though methinks you grudge the act, and I will not run you through the body as I might have done otherwise. For such words as you have just said I like not. Are you wondering how I came to be here with you?"

"They of the Red Brotherhood are like hungry wolves and range everywhere," I answered. "I've yet to sight an island of the Main unpolluted by their cursed feet. So it's no wonder to me to find them here, or to find them marooning each other."

"Marooned? John Gower marooned from his own ship? Scarcely, friend. The craft from which I landed is The Black Raider, on The Account as you know. She sails to intercept a Spanish merchantman and returns in two weeks."

She frowned. "Black be the memory of the day I shipped on her! For a more rascally cowardly crew I have never met. But Roger O'Farrel, my captain aforetime, is without ship at present and I threw in my lot with Gower-the swine! Yesterday he forced me to accompany him ashore, and on the way I gave my opinion of him and his dastardly henchmen. At that they were little pleased and bellowed like bulls, but dared not start fighting in the boat, lest we all fall among the sharks.

"So the moment she beached, I slashed Gower's ape-face with my rapier and out-footed the rest and hid myself. But it was my bad fortune to come upon one alone. He rushed at me and swung with his blade, but I parried it and spitted him with a near riposte just under the heart. Then you came along, Righteousness, and the rest you know. They must have scattered all over the isle, as testifieth Comrel.

"Perhaps I should tell you why John Gower came ashore with seven men. Have you ever heard of the treasure of Mogar?"

"No."

"I thought not. Legend has it that when the Spaniards first sailed the Main, they found an island whereon was a decaying empire. The natives lived in mud and wooden huts on the beach, but they had a great temple of stone, a remnant of some forgotten, older race, in which there was a vast treasure of precious stones. The Dons destroyed these natives, but not before they had concealed their hoard so thoroughly that not even a Spanish nose could smell it out, and those the Dons tortured died unspeaking.

"So the Spaniards sailed away empty-handed, leaving all traces of the Mogar kingdom utterly effaced, save the temple which they could not destroy.

"The island was off the beaten track of ships, and, as time went by, the tale was mostly forgotten, living only as a sailor's yarn. Such men as took the tale seriously and went to the island were unable to find the temple.

"Yet on this voyage, there shipped with John Gower a man who swore that he had set foot on the island and had looked on the temple. He said he had landed there with the French buccaneer de Romber and that they found the temple, just as it was described in the legend.

"But before they could search for the treasure, a man-o-war hove in sight and they were forced to run. Nor ran far ere they fell afoul of a frigate who blew them out of the water. Of the boat's crew who were with de Romber when he found the temple, only this man who shipped with Gower remained alive.

"Naturally he refused to tell the location of it or to draw a map, but offered to lead Gower there in return for a goodly share of the gems. So upon sighting the island, Gower bade his mate, Frank Marker, sail to take a merchantman we had word of some days agone, and Gower himself came ashore-"

"What! Do you mean--"

"Aye! On this very island rose and flourished and died the lost kingdom of Mogar, and somewhere among the trees and vines hereon lies the forgotten temple with the ransom of a dozen emperors!"

"The dream of a drunken sailor," I said uncertainly. "And why tell me this?"

"Why not?" said she, reasonably enough. "We are in the same boat and I owe you a debt of gratitude. W e might even find the treasure ourselves, who knows? The man who sailed with de Romber will never lead John Gower to the temple, unless ghosts walk, for he was Dick Comrel, the man you killed!"

"Listen!" A faint sound had come to me through the dim gurgle of the falls.

Dropping on my belly I wriggled cautiously toward the water-veiled entrance and peered through the shimmering screen. I could make out dimly the forms of five men standing close to the pool. The taller one was waving his arms savagely and his rough voice came to me faintly and as if far away.

I drew back, even though knowing he could not see through the falls, and as I did I felt silky curls brush against my shoulder, and the girl, who had crawled after me, put her lips close to me to whisper, under the noise of the water.

"He with the cut face and the fierce eyes is Captain Gower; the lank dark one is the Frenchman, La Costa; he with the beard is Tom Bellefonte; and the other two are Will Harbor and Mike Donler."

Long ago, I had heard all those names and knew that I was looking on as red-handed and black-hearted a group as ever walked deck or beach. After many gestures and talk which I could not make out, they turned and went along the cliff, vanishing from view.

When we could talk in ordinary tones, the girl said:

"Damme, but Gower is in a rare rage! He will have to find the temple by himself now, since your pistol ball scattered Dick Comrel's brains. The swine! He'd be better putting the width of the Seven Seas between himself and me! Roger O'Farrel will pay him out for the way he has treated me, I wager you, even if I fail in my vengeance."

"Vengeance for what?" I asked curiously.

"For disrespect. He sought to treat me as a woman, not as a buccaneer comrade. When I threatened to run him through, he cursed me and swore he would tame me some day- and made me come ashore with him."

A silence followed, then suddenly she said:

"Zounds! Are we to stay pent up here forever? I'm growing hungry!"

"Bide you here," said I, "and I will go forth and fetch some fruit which grows wild here-"

"Good enough," she replied, "but I crave more than fruit. By Zeus! There is bread and salt pork and dried beef in the longboat and I have a mind to sally forth and-"

Now I, who had tasted no Christian food in more than a week, felt my mouth water at the mention of bread and beef, but I said:

"Are you insane? Of what good is a hiding place if it is not used? You would surely fall into the hands of those rogues."

"No, now is the best time for such an attempt," said she, rising. "Hinder me not-my mind is made up. You saw that the five were together-so there is no one at the boat. The other two are dead."

"Unless the whole gang of them returned to the beach," said I.

"Not likely. They are still searching for me, or else have taken up the hunt for the temple. No, I tell you, now is the best time."

"Then I go with you, if you are so determined," I replied, and together we dropped from the ledge in front of the cavern, splashed through the falls and waded out of the pool.

I peered about, half-expecting an attack, but no man was in sight. All was silent save for the occasional raucous plaint of some jungle bird. I looked to my weapons. One of the dead buccaneer's pistols was empty, of course, and the priming of the other was wet.

"The locks of mine are wrapped in silk," said Helen, noticing my activities. "Here, draw the useless charge and reload them."

And she handed me a waterproof horn flask with compartments for powder and ball. So I did as she said, drying the weapons with leaves.

"I am probably the finest pistol shot in the world," said the girl modestly, "but the blade is my darling."

She drew her rapier and slashed and thrust the empty air.

"You sailors seldom appreciate the true value of the straight steel," said she. "Look at you with that clumsy cutlass. I could run you through while you were heaving it up for a slash. So!"

Her point suddenly leaped out and a lock of my hair floated to the earth.

"Have a care with that skewer," said I, annoyed and somewhat uneasy. "Save your tierces and thrusts for your enemies. As for a cutlass, it is a downright weapon for an honest man who knows naught of your fine French tricks."

"Roger O'Farrel knows the worth of the rapier," said she. "'Twould do your heart good to see it sing in his hand, and how that he spits those who oppose him."

"Let us be going," I answered shortly, for her hardness rasped again on me, and it somehow irked me to hear her sing the praises of the pirate O'Farrel.

So we went silently up through the gorges and ravines, mounting the north cliffs at another place, and so proceeded through the thick trees until we came to the crest of the slope that led down to the beach. Peering from ambush, we saw the longboat lying alone and unguarded.

No sound broke the utter stillness as we went warily down the incline. The sun hung over the western waters tike a shield of blood, and the very birds in the trees seemed to have fallen silent. The breeze had gone and no leaf rustled on any branch.

We came to the longboat and, working swiftly, broke open the kegs and made a bundle of bread and beef. My fingers trembled with haste and nervousness, for I felt we were riding the crest of a precipice-I was sure that the pirates would return to their boat before nightfall, and the sun was about to go down.

Even as this thought came to me, I heard a shout and a shot, and a bullet hummed by my cheek. Mike Donler and Will Harbor were running down the beach toward us, cursing and bellowing horrible threats. They had come upon us from among the lofty rocks further down the shore, and now were on us before we had time to draw a breath.

Donler rushed in on me, wild eyes aflame, belt buckle, finger rings and cutlass blade all afire in the gleam of the sunset. His broad breast showed hairy through his open shirt, and I levelled my pistol and shot him through the chest, so that he staggered and roared like a wounded buffalo. Yet such was his terrible vitality that he came reeling on in spite of this mortal hurt to slash at me with his cutlass. I parried the blow, splitting his skull to the brows with my own blade, and he fell dead at my feet, his brains running out on the sand.

Then I turned to the girl, whom I feared to be hard pressed, and looked just in time to see her disarm Harbor with a dextrous wrench of her wrist, and run him through the heart so that her point came out under his shoulder.

For a fleeting instant he stood erect, mouth gaping stupidly, as if upheld by the blade. Blood gushed from that open mouth and, as she withdrew her sword with a marvelous show of wrist strength, he toppled forward, dead before he touched earth.

Helen turned to me with a light laugh.

"At least Mr. Harmer," quoth she, "my 'skewer' does a cleaner and neater job than does your cleaver. Bones and blades! I had no idea there was so much brain to Mike Donler."

"Have done," said I sombrely, repelled by her words and manner. "This is a butcher's business and one I like not. Let us begone; if Gower and the other two are not behind these, they will come shortly."

"Then take up the pack of food, imbecile," said she sharply. "Have we come this far and killed two men for nothing?"

I obeyed without speaking, though truth to tell, I had little appetite left, for my soul was not with such work as I had just done. As the ocean drank the westering sun and the swift southern twilight fell, we made our way back toward the cavern under the falls. When we had topped the slope and lost sight of the sea except such as glimmered between the trees in the distance, we heard a faint shout, and knew that Gower and the remainder of his men had returned.

"No danger now until morning," said my companion. "Since we know that the rogues are on the beach, there is no chance of coming upon them unexpectedly in the wood. They will scarcely venture into this unknown wilderness at night."

After we had gone a little further, we halted, set us down and supped on the bread and beef, washing it down with draughts from a clear cold stream. And I marveled at how daintily and with what excellent manners this pirate girl ate.

When she had finished and washed her hands in the stream, she tossed her golden curls and said:

"By Zeus, this hath been a profitable day's work for two hunted fugitives! Of the seven buccaneers which came ashore early this morn, but three remain alive! What say you-shall we flee them no more, but come upon them and trust to our battle fortune? Three against two are not such great odds."

"What do you say?" I asked her bluntly.

"I say nay," she replied frankly. "Were it any man but John Gower I might say differently. But this Gower is more than a man-he is as crafty and ferocious as any wild beast, and there is that about him which turns my blood to ice. He is one of the two men I have ever feared."

"Who was the other?"

"Roger O'Farrel."

Now she had a way of pronouncing that rogue's name as if he were a saint or a king, and for some reason this rasped on my nerves greatly. So I said nothing.

"Were Roger O'Farrel here," she prattled on, "we should have naught to fear, for no man on all the Seven Seas is his equal and even John Gower would shun the issue with him. He is the greatest navigator that ever lived and the finest swordsman. He has the manners of a cavalier, which in truth he is."

"Who is this Roger O'Farrel?" I asked brutally. "Your lover?"

At that, quick as a flash, she struck me across the face with her open hand so that I saw stars. We were on our feet, and I saw her face crimson in the light of the moon which had come up over the black trees.

"Damn you!" she cried. "O'Farrel would cut your heart out for that, were he here! From your own lips I had it that no man could call me his!"

"So they say, indeed," said I bitterly, for my cheek was stinging, and my mind was in such a chaotic state as is difficult to describe.

"They say, eh? And what think you?" there was danger in her tone.

"I think," said I recklessly, "that no woman can be a plunderer and a murderess, and also virtuous."

It was a cruel and needless thing to say. I saw her face go white, I heard the quick intake of her breath and the next instant her rapier point was against my breast, just under the heart.

"I have killed men for less," I heard her say in a ghostly, far away whisper.

I looked down at the thin silver line of death that lay between us and my blood froze, but I answered:

"Killing me would scarcely change my opinion."

An instant she stared at me, then to my utter bewilderment, she dropped her blade, flung herself down on the earth and burst into a torrent of sobs. Much ashamed of myself, I stood over her, uncertain, wishing to comfort her, yet afraid the little spitfire would stab me if I touched her. Presently I was aware of words mingling with her tears.

"After all I have done to keep clean," she sobbed. "This is too much! I know I am a monster in the sight of men; there is blood on my hands. I've looted and cursed and killed and diced and drunk, till my very heart is calloused. My only consolation, the one thing to keep me from feeling utterly damned, is the fact that I have remained as virtuous as any girl. And now men believe me otherwise. I wish I. . .I. . . were dead!"

So did I for the instant, until I was swept by an unutterable shame. Certainly the words I had used to her were not the act of a man. And now I was stunned at the removal of her mask of hard recklessness and the revelation of a surprisingly sensitive soul. Her voice had the throb of sincerity, and, truth to tell, I had never really doubted her.

Now I dropped to my knees beside the weeping girl and, raising her, made to wipe her eyes.

"Keep your hands off me!" she ordered promptly, jerking away. "I will have naught to do with you, who believe me a bad woman."

"I don't believe it," I answered. "I most humbly crave pardon. It was a foul and unmanly thing for me to say. I have never doubted your honesty, and I said that which I did only because you had angered me."

She seemed somewhat appeased.

"As for Roger O'Farrel," said she, "he is twice as old as either of us. He took me off a sinking ship when I was a baby and raised me like his own daughter. And if I took to the life of a rover, it is not his fault, who would have established me like a fine lady ashore had I wished. But the love of adventure is in my blood and though Fate made a woman of me, I have lived a man's life.

"If I am hard and cold and heartless, what else might you expect of a maid who grew up among daily scenes of blood and violence, whose earliest remembrances are of sinking ships, crashing cannon and the shrieks of the dying? I know the rotten worth of my companions-sots, murderers, thieves, gallows birds-all save Captain Roger O'Farrel.

"Men say he is cruel and it may be so. But to me he has always been kind and gentle. And moreover he is a fine upstanding man, of high aristocratic blood with the courage of a lion!"

I said nothing against the buccaneer, whom I knew to be the disinherited black sheep of a powerful Irish family, but I experienced a strange sensation of pleasure to learn from her lips just what their relationship was to each other.

A scene long forgotten suddenly flashed in my mind: a boatload of people sighted off the Tortugas and taken aboard- the words of one of the women, "And it's Helen Tavrel we have to thank, God bless her! For she made bloody Hilton put all we a-boat with food and water, when the fiend would ha' burned us all with our ship. Woman pirate she may be, but a kind heart she hath for all that='

After all, the girl was a credit to her sex, considering her raising and surroundings, thought I, and felt strangely cheerful.

"You'll try to forget my words," said I. "Now let us be getting toward our hiding place, for it is like we will have need of it tomorrow."

I helped her to her feet and gave her rapier into her hand. She followed me then without a word and no conversation passed between us until we reached the pool beside the cliff. Here we halted for a moment.

Truth, it was a weird and fantastic sight. The cliffs rose stark and black on either side, and between them whispered and rustled the thick shadows of the fronds. The stream sliding over the cliff before us glimmered like molten silver in the moonlight, and the pool into which it slipped shimmered with long bright ripples. The moon rode over all like a broad buckler of white gold.

"Sleep in the cavern," I commanded. "I will make me a bed among these bushes which grow close by."

"Will you be safe thus?" she asked.

"Aye; no man is like to come before morning, and there are no dangerous beasts on the island, save reptiles which lurk among the swamps on the other side of it."

Without a word, she waded into the pool and vanished in the silver mist of the fall. I parted the bushes near at hand and composed myself for slumber. The last thing I remembered, as I fell asleep, was an unruly mass of golden curls, below which danced a pair of brooding grey eyes.

THE SECOND DAY

Someone was shaking me out of my sound slumber. I stirred, then awoke suddenly and sat up, groping for blade or pistol.

"My word, sir, you sleep deep. John Gower might have stolen upon you and cut out your heart and you not aware of it."

It was hardly dawn and Helen Tavrel was standing over me.

"I had thought to wake sooner," said I, yawning, "but I was weary from yesterday's work. You must have a body and nature of steel springs."

She looked as fresh as if she had but stepped from a lady's boudoir. Truth, there are few women who could endure such exertions, sleep all night on the bare sand of a cavern floor and still look elegant and winsome.

"Let us to breakfast," said she. "Methinks the fare is a trifle scanty, but there is pure water to go with it, and I believe you mentioned fruit?"

Later, as we ate, she said in a brooding manner:

"it stirs my blood most unpleasantly at the thought of John Gower gaining possession of the Mogar treasure. Although I have sailed with Roger O'Farrel, Hilton, Hansen, and le Ban between times, Gower is the first captain to offer me insult."

"He is not like to find it," said I, "for the simple reason that there is no such thing on this island."

"Have you explored all of it?"

"All except the eastern swamps which are impenetrable."

Her eyes lighted.

"Faith, man, were the shrine easy to find, it had been looted long before now. I wager you that it lies somewhere amid that swamp! Now listen to my plan.

"It is yet awhile before sunup and as it is most likely that Gower and his bullies drank rum most of the night, they are not like to be up before broad daylight. I know their ways, and they do not alter them, even for treasure!

"So let us go swiftly to this swamp and make a close search."

"I repeat," said I, "it is tempting Providence. Why have a hiding place if we do not use it? We have been very fortunate so far in evading Gower, but if we keep running hither and yon through the woods we must eventually come on him."

"If we cower in our cave like rats, he will eventually discover us. Doubtless we can explore the swamp and return before he fares forth, or if not---he has nothing of wood craft but blunders along like a buffalo. We can hear them a league off and elude them. So there is no danger in hiding awhile in the woods if need be, with always a safe retreat to run to as soon as they have passed. Were Roger O'Farrel here-"she hesitated.

"If you must drag O'Farrel into it," said I with a sigh, "I must agree to any wild scheme you put forward. Let us be started."

"Good!" she cried, clapping her hands like a child. "I know we will find treasure! I can see those diamonds and rubies and emeralds and sapphires gleaming even now!"

The first grey of dawn was lightening and the east was growing brighter and more rosy as we went along the cliffs and finally went up a wide ravine to enter the thicker growth of trees that ran eastward. We were taking the opposite direction from that taken the day before. The pirates had landed on the western side of the island and the swamp lay on the eastern.

We walked along in silence awhile, and then I asked abruptly:

"What sort of looking man is O'Farrel?"

"A fine figure with the carriage of a king," she looked me over with a critical eye. "Taller than you, but not so heavily built. Broader of shoulder, but not so deep of chest. A cold, strong handsome face, smooth shaven. Hair as black as yours in spite of his age, and fine grey eyes, like the steel of swords. You have grey eyes, too, but your skin is dark and his is very white.

"Still," she continued, "were you shaved and clad properly, you would not cut a bad figure, even beside Captain O'Farrel-how old are you?"

"Twenty-seven."

"I had not thought you that old. I am twenty."

"You look younger," I answered.

"I am old enough in experience," quoth she. "And now, sir, we had best go more silently, lest by any chance there be rogues among these woods."

So we stole cautiously through the trees, stepping over creepers and making our way through undergrowth which rose thicker as we progressed eastward. Once a large, mottled snake wriggled across our path and the girl started and shrank back nervously. Brave as a tigress when opposed to men, she had the true feminine antipathy toward reptiles.

At last we came to the edge of the swamp without having seen any human foe and I halted.

"Here begins the serpent-haunted expanse of bogs and hummocks which finally slopes down into the sea to the east. You see those tangled walls of moss-hung branches and vine-covered trunks which oppose us. Are you still for invading that foul domain?"

The only reply she made was to push past me impatiently.

Of the first few rods of that journey, I like not to remember. I hacked a way through hanging vines and thickly-grown bamboos with my cutlass, and the farther we went, the higher about our feet rose the stinking, clinging mud. Then the bamboos vanished, the trees thinned out, and we saw only rushes towering higher than our heads, with occasional bare spaces wherein green stagnant pools lay in the black, bubbling mud. We staggered through, sinking sometimes to our waists in the water and slime. The girl cursed fervently at the ruin it was making of her finery, while I saved my breath for the labor of getting through. Twice we tumbled into stagnant pools that seemed to have no bottom, and each time were hard put to get back on solid earth- solid earth, said I? Nay, the treacherous shaky, sucking stuff that passed for earth in that foul abomination.

Yet we progressed, ploughing along, clinging to yielding rushes and to rotten logs, and making use of the more solid hummocks when we could. Once Helen set her foot on a snake and shrieked like a lost soul; nor did she ever become used to the sight of them, though they basked on nearly every log and writhed across the hummocks.

I saw no end to this fool's journey and was about to say so, when above the rushes and foul swamp growth about us I saw what seemed to be hard soil and trees just beyond. Helen exclaimed in joy and, rushing forward, promptly fell into a pool which sucked her under except for her nose. Fumbling under the filthy water, I got a good grip on her arms and managed to draw her forth, cursing and spluttering. By that time I had sunk to my waist in the mud about the pool, and it was with some desperation that we fought our way toward the higher earth.

At last our feet felt a semblance of bottom under the mud and then we came out on solid land. Tall trees grew there, rank with vines, and grass flourished high between them, but at least there was no bog. I, who had been all around the swamp's edges, was amazed. Evidently this place was a sort of island, lapped on all sides by the mire. One who had not been through the swamp would think as I had thought: that nothing lay there but water and mud.

Helen was excited, but before she would venture further, she stooped and attempted to wipe some of the mud from her garments and face. Truth, we were both a ludicrous sight, plastered with mire and slime to the eyebrows.

More, in spite of the silk wrappings, water had soaked into Helen's pistols, and mine also were useless. The barrels and locks were so fouled with mud that it would take some time to clean and dry them so they might be recharged from her horn flask, which still contained some powder. I was in favor of halting long enough to do this, but she argued that we were not likely to need them in the midst of the swamp, and that she could not wait-she must explore the place we had found and learn if the temple did in truth stand there.

So I gave in, and we went on, passing between the boles of the great trees, where the branches intertwined so as to almost shut out the light of the sun which had risen sometime before. Such light as filtered through was strange, grey and unearthly, and the tall grass waved through it like thin ghosts. No birds sang there, no butterflies hovered, though we saw several snakes.

Soon we noticed signs of stonework. Sunk in the earth and overgrown by the rank grass lay shattered paves and tiles. Further on, we came to a wide open stretch which was like a street. Great flagstones lay, evenly placed, and the grass grew in the crevices between them. We fell silent as we followed this ancient street, for long-forgotten ghosts seemed to whisper about us, and soon we saw a strange building glimmering through the trees in front of us.

Silently we approached it. No doubt of it; it was a temple, squarely built of great stone blocks. Wide steps led up to its floor, and up these we went, swords drawn, still and awed. On three sides it was enclosed by walls, windowless and doorless; on the fourth by huge, squat columns which formed the front of the edifice. Tiling, worn smooth by countless feet, made up the floor, and in the middle of the great room began a row of narrow steps which led up to a sort of altar. No idol stood there; if there had ever been one, no doubt the Spaniards destroyed it. No carvings decorated wall, ceiling or column. The keynote of the whole was a grim simplicity, a sort of terrible contempt for man's efforts at beautifying and adorning.

What alien people had built that shrine so long ago? Surely some terrible and sombre people who died ages before the brown-skinned Caribs came to rear up their transient empire. (glanced up at the altar which loomed starkly above us. It was set on a sort of platform built solidly from the floor. A column rose from the center of this platform to the ceiling, and the altar seemed to be part of this column.

We went up the steps. For myself, I was feeling not at all at ease, and Helen was silent and slipped her firm little hand into mine, glancing about nervously. A brooding silence hung over the place as if a monster of some other world lurked in the corners ready to leap upon us. The bleak antiquity of the temple oppressed and bore down upon us with a sense of our own smallness and weakness.

Only the quick nervous rattle of Helen's small heels on the stone steps broke the stillness, yet I could picture in my mind's eye the majestic and sombre rites of worship which had been enacted here in bygone years. Now, as we reached the platform and bent over the altar, I saw deep dark stains on its surface and heard the girl shudder involuntarily. More shadows of horror out of the past, and had we known, the horror of that grim shrine was not yet over.

Turning my attention to the solid column which rose behind the altar, my gaze followed it up to the roof. This seemed to be composed of remarkably long slabs of stone, except for the space just above the altar. There a single huge block rested, a stone of completely different character from those of the rest of the temple. It was of a sombre yellowish hue, shot with red veins, and of monstrous size. It must have weighed many tons, and I was puzzled by what means it was held in place. At last I decided that the column which rose from the platform upheld it in some manner, for this entered the ceiling beside the great block. From the ceiling to the platform was, I should say, some fifteen feet, and from the platform to the floor, ten.

"Now that we are here," said the girl, rather breathlessly, "where is the treasure?"

"That's for us to find," I replied. "Before we begin to search, let us prepare our pistols, for the saints alone know what lies before us."

Down the stair we went again, and part way down, Helen halted, an uneasy look in her eyes.

"Listen! Was that a footfall?"

"I heard nothing; it must be your imagination conjuring up noises."

Still she insisted she heard something and was for hurrying out into the open as quickly as might be. I reached the floor a stride or so before her and turned to speak across my shoulder, when I saw her eyes go wide and her hand flew to her blade. I whirled to see three menacing shapes bulking among the columns- three men, smeared with mud and slime, with weapons gleaming in their hands.

As in a dream I saw the fierce burning eyes of John Gower, the beard of the giant Bellefonte, and the dark, saturnine countenance of La Costa. Then they were on us.

How they had kept their powder dry as they crossed that filthy swamp I know not, but even as I drew blade, La Costa fired and the ball struck my right arm, breaking the bone. The cutlass dropped from my numb fingers, but I stooped and, catching it up in my left hand, met Bellefonte's charge. The giant come on like a wild elephant, roaring, his cutlass whirling like a flame. But the desperate fury of a cornered and wounded lion was mine. And, crashing on his guard as a smith hammers an anvil, until the clash of our steel was an incessant clangor, I drove him across the room and beat him to his knees. But he partly parried the blow that felled him, so that my cutlass, glancing from his blade to his skull, turned in my hand and struck flat instead of edgewise, stunning and not killing. At that instant, La Costa clubbed a musket and laid my scalp open so that I fell and lay in my own blood.

Of how Helen fared I was partly told later, and partly saw, dimly, as I lay dazed and unable to rise.

At the first alarum, she had attacked Gower and he had met her with his blade held in a posture for defense rather than attack. Now this Gower was a rare swordsman, able to hold his own for a time against even such a skill. as was Helen's, though his weapon was a heavy cutlass, a blade unsuited for tricky work.

He had no wish to slay her, and he had more craft than to leave himself wide open to her thrust by slashing at her. So he parried her first few tierces, retreating before her while La Costa sought to steal upon her from behind and pinion her arms. Before the Frenchman could accomplish this design, Helen feinted Gower into a wide parry that left him open. Then and there had John Gower died, but luck was not with us that day, and Helen's foot slipped as she thrust for his black heart. The point wavered and only raked his ribs. Before she could recover her balance, Gower shouted and struck down her sword, dropping his own to seize her in his huge arms.

She fought even then, clawing at his face, kicking his shins and striving to shorten her grip on her sword so as to use it against him, but he only laughed. And, having wrenched the rapier out of her hand, he held her helpless as a baby while he bound her with cords. Then he carried her over to a column and, standing her upright against it, made her fast-she raving and cursing in a manner to make one's blood run cold.

Then, seeing that I was struggling to arise, he ordered La Costa to bind me. The Frenchman answered that both my arms were broken. Gower commanded him to bind my legs, which he did, and dragged me over near the girl. And how the Frenchman made this mistake I know not, unless it were that because of the blow on my head, I seemed unable as yet to use my limbs, so he assumed my left arm broken also, besides my right.

"And so, my fine lady," said John Gower in his deep menacing voice, "we end where we began. Where you got this brawny young savage, I know not, but methinks he is in a sad plight. For the present there is work to do, after which I may ease his hurts."

Dazed as I was, I knew that he meant not by saving but by slaying me, and I heard Helen's quick intake of breath.

"You beast!" she cried. "Would you murder the boy?"

Gower gave a cold laugh and turned to Bellefonte, who was just now rising in a muddled sort of way.

"Bellefonte, is your brain yet too addled for our work?"

"Nay," snarled the giant. "But may I roast in Hades if I ever felt such a bash, I would-"

"Get the tools," ordered Gower, and Bellefonte slouched out, to return presently with picks and a great sledge hammer.

"I will tear this cursed building to pieces or find what I look for," quoth John Gower. "As I told you when you asked the reason for loading the sledge into the longboat, my pretty Helen. Comrel died before he could tell us just where this temple lay, but from the hints he had let drop from time to time, I guessed that it lay on the eastern side of the isle. When we came hither this morn and saw the swamp, I felt our search was done. And truth it was, and our search for you also, as I found when I stole up to the columns and peered between them."

"We waste time," broke in Bellefonte. "Let us be tearing down something."

"All a waste of time," said La Costa moodily. "Gower, I say again that this is a fool's quest, bound to end but evilly. This is a haunt of demons; nay, Satan himself hath spread his dark wings o'er this temple and it's no resort for Christians! As for the gems, a legend hath it that the ancient priests of these people flung them into the sea, and I, for one, believe that legend."

"We shall soon see," was Gower's imperturbable reply. "These walls and pillars have a solid look, but persistence and appliance will crumble any stone. Let us to work."

Now strange to say, I have neglected to make mention of the quality of the light in the building. On the outside there was a clear space, no trees growing within several yards of the walls on either side. Yet so tall were those trees which grew beyond this space, and so close their branches, that the shrine lay ever in everlasting shadow, and the light which drifted through between the columns was dim and strange. The corners of the great room seemed veiled in grey mist and the humans moving about appeared like ghosts-their voices sounding hollow and unreal.

"Look about for secret doors and the like," said Gower, beginning to hammer along the walls, and the other two obeyed. Bellefonte was eager, La Costa otherwise.

"No luck will come of this, Gower," the Frenchman. said as he groped in the dimness of afar corner. "This daring of hethen deities in heathen shrines-nom de Dieu!"

We all started at his wild shriek and he reeled from the corner screaming, a thing like a black cable writhing about his arm. As we looked aghast, he crashed down in the midst of the tiled floor and there tore to fragments with his bare hands the hideous reptile which had struck him.

"Oh Heavens!" he screeched, writhing about and staring up at his mates with wild, crazed eyes. "Oh, grand Dieu, I burn, I die! Oh, saints, grant me ease!"

Even Bellefonte's steel nerves seemed shaken at this terrible sight, but John Gower remained unmoved. He drew a pistol and flung it to the dying man.

"You are doomed," said he brutally. "The venom is coursing through your veins like the fire of Hell, but you may live for hours yet. Best end your torment."

La Costa clutched at the weapon as a drowning man seizes a twig. A moment he hesitated, torn between two terrible fears. Then, as the burning of the venom shook him with fierce stabbings, he set the muzzle against his temple,

43

gibbering and yammering, and jerked the trigger. The stare of his tortured eyes will haunt me till Doomsday, and may his crimes on earth be forgiven him for if ever a man passed through Purgatory in his dying, it was he.

"By God!" said Bellefonte, wiping his brow. "This looks like the hand of Satan!"

"Bah!" Gower spoke impatiently. "'Tis but a swamp snake which crawled in here. The fool was so intent upon his gloomy prophesying that he failed to notice it coiled up in the darkness, and so set his hand in its coils. Let not this thing shake you-let us to work, but first look about and see if any more serpents lurk here." ,

"First bind up Mr. Harmer's wounds, if you please," spoke up Helen, a quaver in her voice to tell how she had been affected. "He is like to bleed to death."

"Let him," answered Gower without feeling. "It will save me the task of easing him off."

My wounds, however, had ceased to bleed, and though my head was still dizzy and my arm was beginning to throb, I was nowhere near a dead man. When the pirates were not looking, I began to work stealthily at my bonds with my left hand. Truth, I was in no condition to fight, but were I free, I might accomplish something. So lying on my side, I slowly drew my feet behind me and fumbled at the cords on my ankles with strangely numb fingers. while Gower and his mate poked about in the corner and hammered on the walls and columns.

"By Zeus, I believe yon altar is the key of this mystery," said Gower, halting his work at last. "Bring the sledge and let us have a look at the thing."

They mounted the stair like two rogues going up the gallows steps, and their appearance in the dim light was as men already dead. A cold hand touched my soul and I seemed to hear the sweep of mighty bat-like wings. An icy terror seized me, I know not why, and drew my eyes to the great stone which hung broodingly above the altar. All the horror of this ancient place of forgotten mysteries descended on me like a mist, and I think Helen felt the same for I heard her breath come quick and hard.

The buccaneers halted on the platform and Gower spoke, his voice booming like a hollow mockery in the great room, re-echoing from wall to ceiling.

"Now, Bellefonte, up with your sledge and shatter me this altar." The giant grunted doubtfully at that. The altar seemed merely a solid square of stone, as plain and unadorned as the rest of the fane, an integral part of the platform as was the column behind it. But Bellefonte lifted the heavy hammer and the echoes crashed as he brought it down on the smooth surface.

Sweat gathered on the giant's brow with the effort, and the great muscles stood out on his naked arms and shoulders as he heaved up the sledge and smote again and yet again. Gower cursed, and Bellefonte swore that it was waste of strength cracking a solid rock, but at Gower's urging, he again raised the hammer. He stood with his legs spread wide, arms above his head and bent backward, hands gripping the handle. Then with all his power he brought it down and the hammer handle splintered with the blow; but, with a shattering crash, the whole of the altar gave way and the fragments flew in all directions.

"Hollow, by Satan!" shouted John Gower, smiting fist on palm. "I suspected as much! Yet who would have thought it, with the lid so cleverly joined to the rest that no crack showed at all? Strike flint and steel here, man, the inside of this strange chest is as dark as Hades."

They bent over it and there was a momentary flash, then they straightened.

"No tinder," snarled Bellefonte, flinging aside his flint and steel. "What saw ye?"

"Naught but one great red gem," said Gower moodily. "But it may be that there is a secret compartment below the bottom where it lies."

He leaned over the altar-chest and thrust his hand therein.

"By Satan," said he, "this cursed gem seems to cling fast to the bottom of the chest as though it were fastened to something--a metal rod from the feel- ha, now it gives and-"

Through his words came a muffled creak as of bolts and levers long unused--a rumble sounded from above, and we all looked up. And then the two buccaneers beside the altar gave a deathly cry and flung up their arms as down from the roof thundered the great central stone. Column, altar and stair crashed into red ruin.

Stunned by the terrible earthquake-like noise, the girl and I lay, eyes fixed with terrible fascination on the great heap of shattered stone in the middle of the temple, from under which oozed a river of dark red.

At last after what seemed a long time, I, moving like a man in a trance, freed myself and unbound the girl. I was very weak and she put out an arm to steady me. We went out of that temple of death, and once in the open, never did free air and light seem so fair to me, though the air was tainted with the swamp reek and the light was strange and shadowy.

Then a wave of weakness flooded body and brain; I fell to the earth and knew no more.

AND LAST

Someone was laving my brow and at last I opened my eyes.

"Steve, oh, Steve, are you dead?" someone was saying; the voice was gentle and there was a hint of tears.

"Not yet," said I, striving to sit up, but a small hand forced me gently down.

"Steve," said Helen, and I felt a strange delight in hearing her call me by my first name, "I have bandaged you as well as might be with such material as I had-stuff torn from my shirt. We should get out of this low dank place to a fresher part of the island. Do you think you can travel?"

"I'll try," I said, though my heart sank at the thought of the swamp.

"I have found a road," she informed me. "When I went to look for clean water I found a small spring and also stumbled upon what was once a fine road, built with great blocks of stone set deep in mire. The mud overlaps it now some few inches and rushes grow thereon, but it's passable so let us be gone."

She helped me to my feet and, with one arm about me, guided my uncertain steps. In this manner, we crossed the ancient causeway and I found time to marvel again at the nature of that race who had built so strongly and had so terribly protected their secrets.

The journey through the swamp seemed without end, and again through the thick jungle, but at last my eyes, swimming with torment and dizziness, saw the ocean glimmering through the trees. Soon we were able to sink down beside the longboat on the beach, exhausted. Yet Helen would not rest as I urged her to, but took a case of bandages and ointment from the boat and dressed my wounds. With a keen dagger she found and cut out the bullet in my arm, and I thought I would die thereat, and then made shift at setting the broken bone. I wondered at her dexterity, but she told me that from early childhood she had aided in dressing hurts and setting broken limbs-that Roger O'Farrel tended thus to all his wounded himself, having attended a medical university in his youth, and he imparted all his knowledge to her.

Still she admitted that the setting of my arm was a sad job, with the scant material she had, and she feared it would give me trouble. But while she was talking, I sank back and became unconscious, for I had lost an incredible amount of blood, and it was early dawn of the next day before I came to my full senses.

Helen, while I lay senseless, had made me a bed of soft leaves, spreading over me her fine coat, which I fear was none too fine now, what with the blood and stains on it.

And when I came to myself, she sat beside me, her eyes wide and sleepless, her face drawn and haggard in the early grey of dawn.

"Steve, are you going to live?" asked she, and I made shift to laugh.

"You have scant opinion of my powers if you think a pistol ball and a musket stock can kill me," I answered. "How feel you, Helen?"

"Tired . . . a bit." She smiled. "But remarkably meditative. I have seen men die in many ways, but never a sight to equal that in the temple. Their death shrieks will haunt me to my death. How do you think their end was brought about?"

"All seems mazed and vague now," said I, "but methinks I remember seeing many twisted and broken metal rods among the ruins. From the way the platform and stair shattered, I believe that the whole structure was hollow, like the altar, and the column also. A crafty system of levers must have run through them up to the roof, where the great stone was held in place by bolts or the like. I believe that the gem in the altar was fastened to a lever which, working up through the column, released that stone."

She shuddered.

"Like enough. And the treasure..."

"There never was any. Or if there was, the Caribs flung it into the sea and, knowing some curse lay over the temple, pretended that they had hidden it therein, hoping the Spaniards would come to harm while searching for it. Certainly that thing was not the work of the Caribs, and I doubt if they knew just what sort of fate lay in wait there. But, certes, any man could look on that accursed shrine and instinctively feel that doom overshadowed the place."

"Another dream turned to smoke," sighed she. "La, la, and me a-wishing for rubies and sapphires as large as my fist!"

She was gazing out to sea as she spoke, where the waves were beginning to redden in the glowing light. Now she sprang erect!

"A sail!"

"The Black Raider returning!" I exclaimed.

"No! Even at this distance, I can tell the cut of a man-o'-war! She is making for this island."

"For fresh water, no doubt," said I.

Helen stood twisting her slim fingers uncertainly.

"My fate lies with you. If you tell them I am Helen Tavrel, I will hang between high tide and low, on Execution Dock!"

"Helen," said I, reaching up and taking her small hand and pulling her down beside me, "my opinion of you has changed since first I saw you. I still maintain the Red Trade is no course for a woman to follow, but I realize what circumstances forced you into it. No woman, whatever her manner of life, could be kinder, braver, and more unselfish than you have been. To the men of yonder craft you shall be Helen Harmer, my sister, who sailed with me."

"Two men have I feared," said she with lowered eyes; "John Gower, because he was a beast; Roger O'Farrel, because he was so fine and noble. One man I have respected-O'Farrel. Now I find a second man to respect without fearing. You are a bold, honest youth, Steve, and-"

"And what?"

"Nothing," and she seemed confused.

"Helen," said I, drawing her gently closer to me, "you and I have gone through too much blood and fire together for anything to come between us. Your beauty fascinated me when first I saw you; later I came to understand the sterling worth of the soul which lay beneath your reckless mask. Each soul has its true mate, little comrade, and though I fought the feeling and strove to put it from me, fondness was born in my bosom for you and it has grown steadily. I care not what you may have been, and I am but a sailor, now without a ship, but let me tell yonder seamen when they land that you are, not my sister, but my wife-to-be

A moment she leaned toward me, then she drew away and her eyes danced with the old jaunty fire.

"La, sir, are you offering to marry me? 'Tis very kind of you indeed, but--"

"Helen, don't mock me!"

"Truth, Steve, I am not," said she, softening. "But I had never thought of any such a thing before. La, I must be growing up with a vengeance! Fie, sir, I am too young to marry yet, and I have not yet seen all of the world I wish to. Remember I am still Helen Tavrel."

"I care not; marry me and I will take you from this life."

"Not so fast," said she, tracing patterns in the sand with her finger. "I must have time to think this thing over. Moreover, I will take no step without Roger O'Farrel's consent. I am only a young girl after all, Steve, and I tell you truth, I have never thought of marrying or even having a lover.

"Ah, me, these men, how they press a poor maid!" laughed she.

"Helen!" I exclaimed, vexed yet amused. "Have you no care for me at all?"

"Why, as to that," she avoided my gaze, "I really feel a fondness for you such as I have never felt for any other man, not even Roger O'Farrel. But I must mull over this and discover if it be true love!"

Thereat she laughed merrily aloud, and I cursed despairingly.

"Fie, such language before your lady love!" she said. "Now hear me, Steve, we must seek Roger O'Farrel, wherever he may be, for I am like a daughter to him, and if he likes you, why, who knows! But you must not speak of marrying until I am older and have had many more adventures. Now we shall be true comrades as we have been hitherto."

"And a comrade must allow an honest kiss," said I, glancing seaward where the ship came sweeping grandly.

And with a light laugh she lifted her lips to mine.